D0714609
Charlie
& The Cheese & Onion
Crisps
Withdrawn
30130 149905779

Look out for other books in this series:

Charlie & The Cat Flap

Charlie & The Great Escape

Charlie & The Big Snow

Charlie & The Rocket Boy

Hilary McKay

Illustrated by Sam Hearn

SCHOLASTIC

First published in the UK in 2008
by Scholastic Children's Books
An imprint of Scholastic Ltd
Euston House, 24 Eversholt Street
London, NW1 1DB, UK
Registered office: Westfield Road, Southam, Warwickshire, CV47 0RA
SCHOLASTIC and associated logos are trademarks and or
registered trademarks of Scholastic Inc.

ISBN 978 1407 10364 8

British Library Cataloguing-in-Publication Data
A CIP catalogue record for this book is available from the British Library

Typeset by Falcon
Printed by CPI Bookmarque, Croydon
Papers used by Scholastic Children's Books are made
from wood grown in sustainable forests.

1 3 5 7 9 10 8 6 4 2

www.scholastic.co.uk/zone

No Crisps

It was lunch time at school and Charlie and Henry were sitting together. They always sat together because they were best friends. Charlie and Henry had been best friends for five years, ever since they met on the Naughty Bench at Pre-school.

Nobody understood Henry as well as Charlie did, and nobody understood Charlie as well as Henry did.

So when Charlie said to Henry, "You can have my cheese and onion crisps if you want! They give you such a ponky smell!"

Henry understood at once. "You don't usually mind smelling ponky," he said. "Usually you like them the best! You've gone bonkers again, haven't you?"

Charlie smiled and did not say he hadn't.

"Who is it this time?" demanded Henry. "No, don't tell me! I can guess! It's the new student teacher that came this morning!"

Charlie's smile got worse than ever, and he gazed across the dining hall at the new student teacher.

"What's her name?" asked Henry. "I wasn't listening when she said."

Charlie shrugged. He hadn't been listening either. He didn't think her name mattered. She was simply the New Miss, fascinating and lovely because she had long red curly hair and a leather thong round her neck with a stone threaded on to it.

"I can't see anything special about her," said Henry, "she gets ratty dead easy and she looks like a witch. That stone round her neck is just a normal boring stone."

"I know. I heard her tell Lulu she found it on the beach."

"That's not a good reason to wear it round her neck," said Henry. "I found a dead seal on the beach once..."

"You've told me a million times!"

"...A *huge* dead seal..."

"Seals aren't that huge," objected Charlie.

"They look much bigger dead than they do in zoos. Parts of it had been chewed or something. It smelled a bit like..." (Henry glanced into Charlie's lunch box) "...ham sandwiches and a bit like it had died of old age..."

"I don't know why you're telling me all this *again*!" groaned Charlie.

"I'm just explaining that it definitely wasn't the sort of thing you'd want to wear round your neck... "

Charlie picked the ham out of his sandwich and pushed it down Henry's collar. A dinner lady caught him ham-handed and

sent him to stand by the wall. Henry trailed after him because they were friends and they continued gazing at the New Miss.

"Rubbish shoes," remarked Henry.

"Girls," said Charlie, "only ever look good in very high heels or roller skates. I don't see why they don't just wear them all the time. I would."

"You'd fall over all the time then."

"I wouldn't," said Charlie, rolling his eyes at Henry's silliness, "because I'd be a *girl*! Dope!"

Henry fished a bit of ham up from under his collar and ate it. He did not bother to argue any more. He knew it would be no good. Falling in love did weird things to Charlie's brain. Now (like countless times before) he would give up cheese and onion crisps, try and teach himself football tricks, spend a great deal of time smiling and leaning against walls, and arrange his hair in unnatural formations of swirls and spikes with hair gel borrowed from Henry's vast hair gel collection.

There was only one good thing about Charlie in love.

"It never lasts long," said Henry thankfully.

Lunch ended, Henry and Charlie went

outside and the New Miss went back to the classroom. Charlie practised football tricks as close to the window as he dared while

Henry kept an eye on her through the glass and from time to time said helpfully, "She's not watching ... good job she didn't see that ... she's still not watching..."

The New Miss did not survive the afternoon. First she ruined Art by handing out paper plates and demanding they all draw healthy salads and then she gave out worksheets about Henry the Eighth with pictures of all of his six unfortunate wives.

"Label the wives and colour them in," she ordered.

Charlie gave all six red floppy hair and stones round their necks and the New Miss put his worksheet in the recycling bin.

"I hope you are not trying to be rude," she said.

Charlie, who could be much ruder than

that without trying at all, was very offended indeed.

Henry was right; he decided, she did look like a witch.

"I should like to meet someone *perfect*," he said as he walked home with Henry, and he described his perfect girl to Henry. Henry was not a bit surprised to hear that she would have floppy hair and sticky out plaits and her neck would be hung with interesting things on strings. Also she would be a whiz on a skateboard or roller blades or very high heels.

"And," said Charlie, tossing his Art into a nearby bin, "she will never eat salad!"

"Salad *is* good for you," said Henry. "Look at elephants."

"Yes, look at elephants!" said Charlie.

"They are fat and wrinkly and nearly extinct!"

"I'll tell my mum that," said Henry, very impressed. "She's been saying look at elephants and making me eat salad for years!"

"You tell her then," said Charlie.

"I will," said Henry, and he did, while Charlie stood around nodding helpfully.

"Look at elephants!" cried Henry's mother, vacuuming around them as if they were furniture. "Whenever am I supposed to get time to look at elephants, may I ask?" and she shooed them upstairs with an apple and a satsuma each and two tubes of smarties because it was Friday.

They gobbled up their apples and exploded their satsumas and agreed to save the Smarties for a little bit later when

Charlie would teach Henry the Truly Amazing Smarties Trick (at which he was almost perfect). After that they gelled up their hair into gravity defying banana-scented spikes with Henry's latest hair gel (Tropical Fruits Extra Firm Hold) and

Henry described *his* perfect girl to Charlie. And she was going to be so very, very rich that she would insist on giving Henry at least a million pounds just to save her the bother of looking after it.

And then she would go and live on the other side of the world.

The moment Henry took delivery of the cash.

"Admit she sounds perfect," said Henry smugly.

Charlie said she didn't sound real.

"Neither does yours," said Henry, and

then they went back into the street to check their spikes would stay up in the wind, and Henry said, "Crikey!"

Because there she was.

Charlie's perfect girl.

Coming down the street with Charlie's big brother Max.

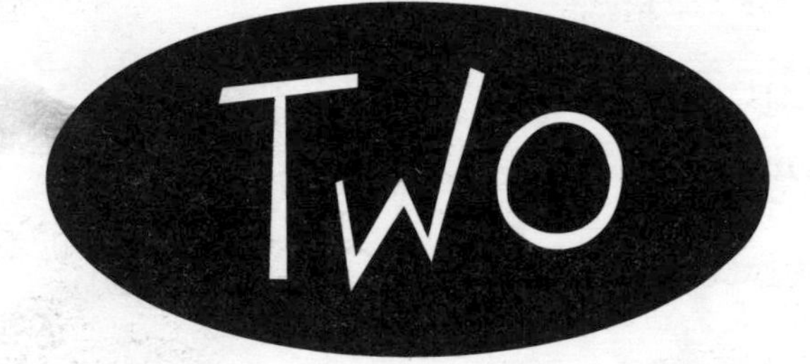

Quite A Lot of Smarties

The Perfect Girl was in school uniform, and she made it look like the coolest clothes in the world. Her huge school uniform shirt almost covered her tiny school uniform skirt. Her school uniform tie had been transformed into a belt. A denim backpack swung from one shoulder and two sticky-out blonde plaits bounced from under a heap of blonde floppy hair. Around her neck were silver chains, strings of shells and a large blue stone on a leather thong. She did not walk, she glided and spun as if she was on wheels.

She *was* on wheels; she wore white wheelie trainers.

She floated along the pavement, sometimes a little ahead, sometimes backwards talking and shaking her plaits, but she kept coming back to Max.

"It is NOT FAIR!" wailed Charlie.

*

It never was fair with Max. He was four years older than Charlie, and it seemed to Charlie that he had been born with Charlie's share of good luck as well as his own.

Max was very nearly a teenager and so tall he looked even older than that. He was good at everything. He could whistle through his fingers, raise one eyebrow and juggle with a football. He could swing from the crossbars of the swings in the park, do running dives into the swimming pool and ride a bike with no hands. He grew so quickly his clothes did not get time to wear out and then Charlie, who never seemed to grow at all, had to wear them for ever.

There were times when Charlie could hardly bear his big brother Max.

Max and Charlie's perfect girl had paused on their way. She had pointed to a notice fastened to a lamp post, and they had read it together. Charlie and Henry saw the Perfect Girl smiling and nodding. They saw Max shrug and move away. They were getting closer and closer but they did not seem to see Charlie bobbing up and down on the pavement.

In fact, they both kept glancing backwards.

"What'll I do to make her notice me?"

wailed Charlie and almost at once found the answer in his hand.

The Truly Amazing (Nearly Perfect) Smarties Trick.

The Truly Amazing (Nearly Perfect) Smarties Trick had another name: Drinking Smarties. The performer held a tube of Smarties high above his open mouth and drank them as they poured.

It was a wonder of breathing and swallowing and timing.

Max and the Perfect Girl were only a few steps away.

Charlie pulled open his Smarties tube, and tipped back his head.

Rattle, rattle, rattle, went the stream of Smarties into Charlie's open mouth, and vanished.

It really was spectacular.

It was a five second multicoloured miracle. Not a single Smarties missed. It was Charlie's most successful performance ever.

Henry applauded, Max looked disgusted

and the girl on wheelie trainers who had missed the whole thing asked, "What?"

"Me!" squeaked Charlie. "Watch properly this time!" and he grabbed Henry's tube of Smarties.

"OY!" shouted Henry, but too late. Charlie was beginning the whole trick all over again.

It should have worked but it didn't. Henry's shout put Charlie off so that the whole drinking and breathing and timing thing was ruined.

Charlie choked like an explosion and a volcanic eruption of Smarties shot from his face and showered his astonished audience.

"What a waste! What a waste!" yelled Henry, scurrying round gathering up his property.

"OUUFFF!" went Charlie, and hurled

another rain of Smarties into the air.

"Stop it! Stop it!" complained Henry furiously.

"He'll die!" announced the Perfect Girl. "He's choking! He'll die!"

"He'll not," said Max grumpily. "He's my brother. I've seen him do it thousands of times before. He's just disgusting."

"WHARRRGGGHHH!!!!!" said Charlie, erupting again.

"Do something!" the girl ordered Max, so Max picked Charlie up, hoisted him upside down and shook him. A stream of Smarties tumbled out like pennies from a piggy bank and Charlie stopped choking and went suddenly boneless.

"That was the most amazing thing I ever saw!" said the Perfect Girl, gazing round at the constellations of Smarties still ungathered by Henry. "How many do you think he ate? Shouldn't someone be taking care of him?"

"I just did," said Max, lowering Charlie not very gently on to the pavement and beginning to move quickly away.

"Does he do it *often*?" asked the Perfect Girl, hurrying after him.

"Yes. Quite."

"They're both gathering up Smarties now!"

"Probably going to eat them."

"The one that's your brother is smiling at me. I love his hair! He must have done it himself..."

Max grunted and walked a bit faster. They were quite far away now but the voice of the Perfect Girl came floating back, laughing and clear.

"He really is kind of cute..."

*

Charlie suddenly came alive with happiness.

"It worked!" he cried, punching Henry joyfully. "Did you hear what she said? Cute! She said cute! How about that?"

"Oh fantastic," said Henry sourly. "Are you sitting on any more Smarties?"

"Loads!"

"I'm having all mine back!'

"OK. I only borrowed them."

"Borrowed them and swallowed them!"

"Just for a minute," said Charlie soothingly. "What did you think Henry, when you heard her say I was cute?"

"I thought she was bonkers," said Henry.

Skateboard Tricks

"So," said Charlie to Henry on Saturday morning. "What'll I do next? Now that I've got her thinking that I'm cute and everything?"

"Why don't you ask Max?" asked Henry. "He should know. He likes her too."

They were in the park at the time, the little green park just along the street from their houses. Their mothers had decided that this summer they were allowed to be there on their own. After all, it was so close that you could see it from the windows of Charlie's house, and the road in between was very quiet.

"They ought to be safe," said Charlie and Henry's mothers.

Charlie and Henry did not feel very safe that Saturday morning. They were taking turns with Henry's skateboard which they had recklessly oiled before they came out. Oiling had transformed it. Before only two of the wheels moved at all. Now all four of them spun at a touch. Charlie and Henry hardly dared step on it.

"Maybe we should gunge it up again," suggested Charlie. "And Max doesn't like

her. He's not bothered about her at all. He told me."

"Ho!" said Henry disbelievingly, and looked across the park. Gemma was in the little one's playground, carefully pushing someone's toddler on one of the baby swings. A group of Max's friends were taking turns to vault a bench. Max was all by himself, not quite in the little one's playground because no footballs were allowed there, but very nearby. He was doing fantastic football tricks. He could bounce the ball from his knees to his head, catch it on his shoulders, slide it down his back, and hook it up with his foot all in one easy movement. It was lovely to watch, but no one was looking except Charlie and Henry.

"He's got his hair gelled up just like yours," said Henry. "And he's looking at

her just the way you looked at the New Miss on Friday."

"The way I looked at who?"

"The New Miss," said Henry. "Floppy hair! Awful shoes! Half a dead seal round her neck!"

"Oh her," said Charlie, stepping very carefully with one foot on to the skateboard, "Look, I'm doing it Henry! I'm balanced!"

"Make it move then!"

Charlie scooted forward the smallest amount possible and stayed triumphantly upright.

"Woo hoo!" he sang, glided at least six inches and waved boldly to Gemma.

Gemma smiled and waved back.

This was too much for Charlie. His arms flailed in frantic

windmill circles and he toppled over backwards into a flower bed.

Gemma's eyebrows flew up and she raised a hand to her mouth.

"I'm all right! I'm all right!" cried Charlie, bouncing to his feet and racing across the grass to the swings with Henry stumping along behind him. "I'm actually very tough, aren't I Henry? I really like your pink hat! D'you mind if I look at your trainers? Did you know you've got my favourite sort of hair? I heard what you said about me yesterday, you know!"

"What did I say?" asked Gemma.

"You said I was cute!"

"Did I?"

"You know you did!" said Charlie, attempting a somersault over a baby swing and landing at her feet.

"Well," said Gemma (who had delicious dimples both sides of her mouth), "so you are!"

And she reached down with both hands and pulled him up again.

A football shot like a comet past Charlie's left ear, close enough for him to feel the whoosh of air as it passed. A flying figure sped across the grass, leaped on to Henry's abandoned skateboard, rode it in a tremendous screeching curve down the path, jumped the three steps down to the gate (landing perfectly, crouched and balanced like a cat) and vanished beyond the bushes between the park and the road.

Moments later the skateboard came sailing into view.

It landed with a flump on the grass.

"Max," said Henry, "does not think that Charlie is cute."

Bm9 x Chaz

A few minutes later Charlie arrived home and bounced up the stairs to the room he shared with his brother. There was a big sulky lumpy bump on the top bunk that belonged to Max.

"There you are!" said Charlie in a pleased happy voice. "I looked for you everywhere downstairs. Did you see me with Gemma?"

The bump on the bed lashed out with a sudden foot.

"I'm going to make her a card to say Happy New House because she's just moved to a new house. So is it OK if I borrow your new felt pens because I don't know where you hid them?"

The bump growled.

"And some of your card if you don't

mind and could you fold it in half because I can never do it neat enough?"

The bump gave a big sigh.

"And then I'll go away."

The bump on the bed rolled on to the floor and turned into Max. Max pulled his sleeping bag out of the bottom of the wardrobe and reached his new felt pens down from the top. He took a sheet of cardboard from his school art folder. He folded the card very neatly in half.

"That's perfect," said Charlie.

Max opened up the top of the sleeping bag and slid the felt pens and card inside. After that he picked up Charlie and scrunched him into a ball and dropped him into the sleeping bag too. He shook it so that all the junk settled at the bottom and he twisted the top closed. Then he heaved the whole bundle on to his shoulder, carried it out of the room and dropped it down the stairs.

Charlie tumbled and rolled down the stairs, across the hall, out of the open front door and into the garden where his mother and Gemma were talking over the gate.

"...Saving up for a karaoke machine," he heard Gemma say he slowed down. "I love little kids! *Goodness*!"

"Hullo Gemma!" said Charlie, crawling out of the sleeping bag.

"What *happened* to you?" asked Gemma, and at the same time Charlie's mother demanded, "*Now* what have you done to Max?"

"Nothing," said Charlie, glaring scarily at his mother and smiling even more scarily at Gemma, and marched off to make his card. On the front he wrote Happy New House over a very bright picture that used every one of Max's new felt pens. Inside he added the other thing he wanted to say. Under a large red glowing heart with sharp black arrows shooting through it he wrote:

B m9

X

Chaz

It looked so good that he took it round to Henry's house for Henry to admire.

"How's she going to know what it means?" asked Henry. "Chaz? What's Chaz?"

"Chaz is just a cool way of saying Charlie," explained Charlie.

"And what's be-M-nine?"

"Be *mine*," said Charlie. "*Be mine*, it says."

"Then X marks the spot?"

"*NO*! That's a ... oh, never mind!"

"I only asked," said Henry primly,

"because if it's not X marks the spot it looks a bit like it could be a kiss so you might want to change it. How are you going to give it to her?"

"I thought you could."

"*Me*? Why me?"

"Because," said Charlie, "you're my best friend."

That was true, Henry was Charlie's best friend.

"She's in the park right now, with someone's kid. She loves little kids. I heard her telling my mum."

"Oh all right," agreed Henry and he stomped away with the card to find Gemma.

She was see-sawing a borrowed toddler and looking very bored indeed.

Henry, who quite liked babies offered,

"D'you want me to go on that see-saw with him? I could give him dead good bumps."

"No thanks."

"Push him on the swings?" suggested Henry, and passed him a packet of bubblegum sweets so he could help himself. The toddler stuffed a fistful into his mouth and overflowed with pink drool.

"You musn't give them stuff!" protested Gemma, as she grabbed him and hung him over the bin.

"Sorry. I came to bring you this. "

"What?" asked Gemma, plucking off the toddler's hat, mopping his face with the pompom and plonking it back on again.

"Oh, a card. Thank you! Is it from you?"

"NO!"

"Who then?"

"You have to work it out."

"Who gave it to you to give to me?" she asked cunningly.

"Ah ha!" said Henry, now at the top of the climbing frame. "Look! No hands!"

The toddler looked in admiration and began climbing frantically towards him.

"Just let go!" said Henry encouragingly. "That's right! Now the other one ... or are your legs too short?"

The toddler tumbled into Gemma's arms and knocked her off her wheels. The roars were tremendous.

"Legs too short," diagnosed Henry suddenly losing interest, and went home.

Charlie, watching the whole thing through the landing window, had sighed with satisfaction when he saw Gemma open her card.

"Now she knows," he said.

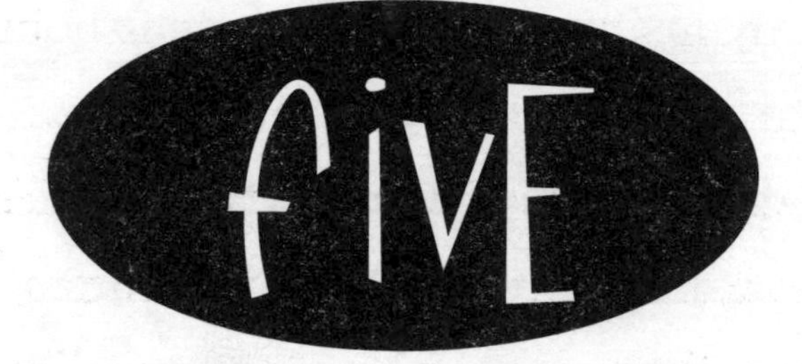

The Only Thing Max Couldn't Do

Max was behaving very oddly.

He was moaning about his trainers.

And trying on all his T-shirts.

He even cut slits in his new jeans and carefully frayed the edges.

"Mum will kill you," said Charlie, watching.

Also he spent a lot of time just staring

at himself in the mirror.

"What do I look like from the back?" he asked Charlie once.

"You look the same as you do from the front," said Charlie. "Only without a face."

A day or two later Charlie came in from the garden and heard music playing upstairs. When he crept up to investigate, there was Max.

At first Charlie thought he was doing exercises to music.

And then he thought he was trying to wriggle out of his shirt to music.

Or to reach an itch to music.

And then he realized that what Max was doing was trying to dance.

That was very odd, because Max did not approve of dancing. He always made excuses, saying things like, "I have leg ache/ I have homework/ My bedroom needs tidying/ I am watching this programme/ Reading this book/ Very busy with this cat..."

Or sometimes, simply, "I wouldn't be seen dead..."

Not a bit like Charlie, who together with Henry had been livening up dance floors since he was three years old. Charlie and Henry loved discos. They would dance with anyone, sing along to any song, and consume anything left lying on the refreshment table.

While Charlie was watching Max his favourite song in all the world came on the radio and he could not resist joining in.

*

"*HEY*! (Hey!) *You*! (You!) *Get Off of My Cloud*!" sang Charlie, doing big stomps, and playing air guitar with his eyes shut and leaning backwards which he knew, because Henry had told him, looked cooler than the coolest of cool.

"Don't hang around 'cos two's a crowd!"

Suddenly the music was switched off, and

Max was asking, "How do you do it?"

"What?" asked Charlie, opening his eyes.

"Did you see anyone and copy? Did someone actually show you? Is that the sort of stuff you and Henry do when you go to discos?"

For a few moments Charlie's head whirled. Always in the past it had been Charlie asking Max a million questions about something that seemed to everyone else to be as easy as breathing.

"I only asked," said Max, "because I may have to go to a disco and I think when I am there I may have to ... may have to ... may have to..."

"Dance?"

"Yes, and you seem to be able to! Anyway, you don't go red and you don't keep stopping..."

Was this really Max? wondered Charlie. The Max who had taught him to blow bubble gum bubbles, ride a bike, slide the fireman's pole in the park and make squeakers out of blades of grass. Was he joking?

It was Max, and he wasn't joking.

Charlie felt suddenly very old and wise and successful. He felt like the grown up big brother, with Max for the useless little one.

For the next half an hour he tried very patiently to teach Max how to dance.

It was very, very hard.

"You have to move your arms and legs," said Charlie. "Pretend you are playing the drums! Or a guitar like me! Sing the words! Make them up if you don't know them! Try not looking at your feet for a bit!"

"Anyway," said Charlie, encouragingly

(although nothing had improved and it seemed, incredibly, that the only thing Max couldn't do was the only thing he, Charlie, could), "they'll play slow dances at the end. They are much easier. You just rush to the prettiest girl in the room (you may have to push a few people out of the way), and say 'I'm dancing this with you' and grab her and don't let go..."

Then Max, who was not scared of ghosts, or heights, or any ride at the fair,

Max who would fetch a ball from anyone's garden, jump into any depth of water and had once actually spoken in French to a French person, Max the bravest of the brave, looked utterly terrified.

"Grab them?" he asked.

"Yep."

"What if they won't come?"

"Pull harder."

"I mean, what if they say 'No!'"

"They never say no," said Charlie, "they are grateful, Max!"

Max's Big Night Out

"Guess what my brother Max is doing tonight!" said Charlie on Friday night as he and Henry walked home together.

"Bashing you up again?"

"No."

"Trying out for the England team?"

"Not yet."

"Not the fourteen Weetabix challenge?"

"No, he's still stuck on twelve. After that he chokes."

"Give up then."

"Going to that disco."

Henry snorted in disbelief.

"He is too! He's going back from school with his friend Greg and they're getting changed and going together. I helped him choose what to wear."

"You!"

"Yes. AND I taught him how to dance like we do."

"What, all our pretend guitar playing and everything?"

"Yep."

"Can he do it?"

"No."

Henry smirked.

"But it doesn't matter because I've told

him all about slow dances and all that. And how to get a girl."

"What girl?"

"Yes well, he wouldn't tell me that."

"Gemma."

"Not Gemma," said Charlie. "He doesn't even like Gemma! He doesn't even think she's pretty! He told me."

"She is though," said Henry.

"Gemma," said Charlie sternly, "is mine!"

They had reached Henry's gate. Charlie opened it for Henry like he was twenty one and Henry was six. This made Henry very mad and he said, "I can open my own gate *thank you*, and as a matter of fact I saw Gemma before you did."

"What?"

"I may ask her to go out with *me*," said

Henry, deliberately being as aggravating as possible. "If Max doesn't want her and you're too scared!"

"I'm not scared."

"Ask her then! I dare you!"

"I will."

"When?"

"When I want to."

"Ha! You won't! Double dare!"

Charlie marched off down the street, pushed open the door of his house and vanished inside. The telephone rang.

"Double dare with knobs on!"

Charlie slammed the phone down and went to fume in his bedroom.

After a while his mum came and found him.

"We have a problem," she said. "What am I going to do with you this evening, with your dad working late and Max out and me with my yoga class? I suppose I will have to take you with me."

She groaned.

Charlie groaned too because he did not fit in very well with his mother's yoga class.

"Last time you said never again," he reminded her.

"Yes, well I often say never again and end up doing it," said Charlie's mother, "and by the way Henry has just telephoned with a very strange message. He said to tell you Yellow Knobs."

Charlie growled, grabbed a handful of lime-flavoured hair gel, rubbed his hair into lime-flavoured tentacles and dashed out of the room.

"Where are you going?" shouted his mother.

"To see a girl."

"What girl?"

"Gemma."

"That's a very good idea," said Charlie's mother, but Charlie had already disappeared.

"Yellow Knobs to you," he said to Henry, some time later. "Please don't offer me any cheese and onion crisps or anything ponky like that because I have a Big Night in with Gemma. She is coming over for pizza and then we are watching a DVD!"

"Oh!" exclaimed Henry jealously, "Oh, it's not fair, having pizza without me! I never have pizza without you. I bet it's pepperoni as well! What DVD are you watching?"

"I'm not telling you because you'd be upset."

"I may have fallen in love with Gemma too!" shouted Henry. "I *did* see her before you did!"

"But," said Charlie, shaking his lime-flavoured tentacles very annoyingly, "did she see you? Anyway, it's your fault! You dared me!"

"OK," said Henry. "Now I'll dare you something else then! I dare you to ask her to marry you!"

"*What?*"

"Double dare! With..."

"Of course I will," said Charlie. "No problem!"

Charlie's Big Night In

Oh, thought Charlie, later that evening, Gemma is *lovely*!

She and his mother had met at the front gate; Gemma had come in as his mother went out. She had glided right up to him, kicked off her wheelies, and given him a delicious, bubblegum-scented hug. While he tried out her wheelies she had sat on the doorstep and painted her toenails blue. They ate the pizza on the doorstep too. Sharing a pizza with Gemma, Charlie found, was a very different experience to sharing with Henry or Max. There were no cross words about which was the biggest slice or who had the most pepperoni.

"I don't really like pepperoni," said Gemma, and flicked hers into the bushes. She didn't eat her crusts either, and she daintily picked off all the mushroom too. After her second slice she left the rest to Charlie. He finished it while she hummed dreamily and told him all about the karaoke machine she planned to buy.

After the pizza Gemma ate three low fat yoghurts because she was on a diet and Charlie didn't, because he wasn't, and then they settled on the sofa together to watch the DVD.

"In real life," said Gemma, nodding at the swashbuckling captain of the pirate ship, "he looks a lot like you!"

"Like me?"

"Definitely. With the right make-up you'd look just like him. I'll show you if you like."

"When? Now? I've got a pirate hat!"

"Come on then!" said Gemma.

*

It took a while, and a lot of Charlie's mum's make-up, but it was worth it.

"See!" said Gemma when they were back on the sofa again with the DVD running, and the lights turned low. "Told you so! Exactly like him, except for the hair."

"I'll grow my hair," said Charlie huskily, "Gemma?"

"Mmm?"

"When I'm sixteen how old will you be?"

"Twenty."

"Do you want to marry me then?"

"Yeah, all right," said Gemma.

"Wait till I tell Henry!" said Charlie.

"That was the easiest ever!"

"Easiest what?"

"Nothing," said Charlie, putting an arm round her.

"Dead cute," said Gemma.

Then everything was ruined.

Bash! went the front door and it was Max.

Stamp! Stamp! Stamp! went Max down the hall, crashed into the living room and flicked on the lights. Charlie, comfortably slumped against Gemma and looking exactly like a pirate hero except for his hair, blinked in surprise.

"Hiya!" said Gemma in a very little voice.

"OH!" exclaimed Max. "YOU! YOU'RE HERE! I MIGHT HAVE KNOWN! I MIGHT HAVE KNOWN! *GOODBYE*!"

"He's a bit weird," said Charlie, and he

tried to snuggle back down again but the magic was gone.

"I'd better go," said Gemma, looking at her watch. "Two hours ... two and a half ... call it three ... I'll just write a little note..."

"You're not really going?" pleaded Charlie.

But she was. She was pulling on her wheelie trainers and pushing a little pink note in his hand. She rushed out of the house so fast she bumped into his mum coming in. She called, "Bye Charlie darling!" and vanished.

The evening was over and it was Max's fault and Charlie marched upstairs to tell him so.

Max was face down on his bed and he was fuming.

"....learning that horrible dancing..." Charlie heard, "...putting that gunk on my hair and being scared all day! And it cost two pounds! Two pounds to be tortured! And it was her idea! It was all her idea! Hanging around and hanging around and waiting and waiting! She *said* she'd be there! She promised! And in the end I had to go up to her two stupid friends and they thought I was asking them to dance and I had to explain that I wasn't and then do you know what they said?"

"What?"

"THEY SAID SHE'D GOT A LAST MINUTE BABYSITTING JOB!"

"Oh."

"*AND IT WAS YOU!*"

"Me?" said Charlie, "Me? Are you mad? 'Course it wasn't me! I've been with Gemma the whole time..."

And then he looked down at the pink

paper he was holding in his hand.

And unfolded it.

It was very pretty. She had dotted her "i"s with little tiny hearts.

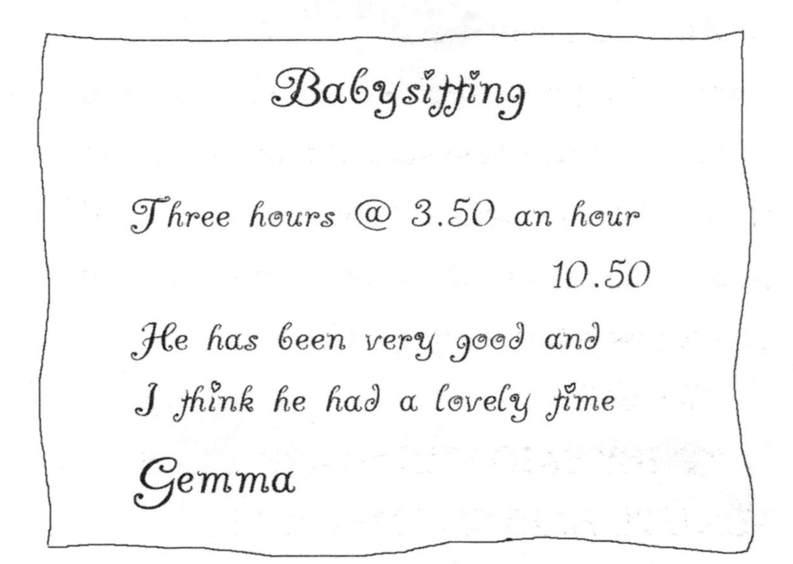
Babysitting

Three hours @ 3.50 an hour
10.50

He has been very good and
I think he had a lovely time

Gemma

"AAARGGHHH!" yelled Charlie, flinging the hateful pink paper on the floor and jumping on it with both feet. "Rotten girl! Her and her wheelies! Her and her plaits! Babysitting! Do I look like a baby?"

He stared at Max, fists clenched and raging, with rivers of pirate make up pouring down his cheeks.

Max stared back.

"STOP LAUGHING! IT'S NOT FUNNY!"

"I'm not laughing," said Max, and he wasn't. He knew too well how Charlie felt.

"What'll I tell Henry?" snuffled Charlie, and buried his head in his arms. He was suddenly very tired of being in love.

Then Max took charge, like he always used to do in a crisis.

"Wait there!" said Max.

"He saved my life!" Charlie to Henry the next morning. "Max did. When I fainted..."

"Fainted?"

"...with sadness and he saved my life by wafting crisps round my head till I revived ... cheese and onion. They're making me better. This is the fourth bag I've had since last night. She's mad, you know?"

"Gemma is?"

"Guess what she said when I asked her to marry me?"

"What?"

"She said, 'Yeah all right'"

"She's mad," agreed Henry.

"Blue feet she's got and she won't eat pepperoni. Low fat yoghurt, that's what she likes."

"Yuk!"

"And my mum says she either can't count or can't tell the time ... anyway, we're over her, Max and me, and we're going swimming after school tonight. Max said he'd take me..."

"Oh!" said Henry jealously.

"And he said you can come too, if your mum says yes."

"She'll say yes," said Henry, skipping with pleasure, "because she likes Max. She's says he's responsible. And grown up. Grown up and responsible! Can you drink crisps like you can Smarties?"

"No," said Charlie, "but I can balance them on my nose and lick them off with my tongue! Max showed me how last night."

"Cheese and onion?"

"Any flavour!"

"Sounds a bit ponky!"

"Who cares about ponky?" asked Charlie. "Not Max and me!"

Meet Charlie – he's trouble!

Charlie's fed up with his mean family always picking on him – so he's decided to run away. That'll show them! Now they'll be sorry!

But running away means being boringly, IMPOSSIBLY quiet…

Meet Charlie – he's trouble!

"The snow's all getting wasted! What'll we do? It will never last till after school!"

Charlie's been waiting for snow his whole life, but now it's come, everyone's trying to spoil it! Luckily, Charlie has a very clever plan to keep it safe...